SCHOOL SIDEKICKS

FRIENDS ALL DAY

by Molly Beth Griffin

illustrated by Colin Jack

PICTURE WINDOW BOOKS
a capstone imprint

TABLE OF CONTENTS

SCHOOL SIDEKICKS

These five friends live within the walls,
nooks, and crannies of an elementary school.
They learn alongside kids every day,
even though the kids don't see them!

STELLA

Stella is a mouse. She loves her
friends. She also loves children and
school! She came into the school on
a cold winter day. She knew it would
be her home forever. Her favorite
subjects are social studies and music.
She is always excited for a new day.

BO

Bo is a parakeet. He is a classroom
pet. The friends let him out of his
cage so they can play together.
Bo loves to read. He goes home
with his teacher on weekends,
but he always comes back to
school to see his friends.

DELILAH

Delilah is a spider. She has always lived in the corners of the school. She is so small the children never notice her, but she is very smart. Delilah loves math and computers and hates the broom.

NICO

Nico is a toad. He used to be a classroom pet. A child forgot to put him back into his tank one day. Now he lives with his friends. The whole school is his home! He can be grumpy, but he loves science and art. Since Nico doesn't have fingers, he paints with his toes!

GOLDIE

Goldie is a goldfish. She is very wise. The friends ask her questions when they have a big choice to make. She gives good advice and lives in the media center.

Chapter 1

THE BEGINNING

Brinnnnnng! Stella the Mouse woke with a jump. The first bell! She'd almost missed the best part of the day!

She scampered down the hall to the front doors. She pressed her little nose against the cold glass. YES! There they were. The big yellow buses with children spilling out.

Stella loved children. She did not like how quiet the school was without them. She also did not like how still and dark the school was at night. Now the halls were bright and loud.

Stella ran to get her best friends. She met up with Nico the Toad and Delilah the Spider first. Then the three friends picked up Bo the Parakeet.

They watched and waited as the children rushed past. Then they scampered and hopped and crept out from their hiding place.

Some of the children ate breakfast before class. Stella and her friends were hungry too! They headed to the cafeteria.

They dipped and darted around the children's feet, grabbing spilled food. With full bellies, they went to class.

The friends liked different subjects. Stella liked social studies. Nico liked science. Delilah liked math. Bo liked reading.

They were sneaky. The friends did not let the children see them. They peeked out from behind trash cans.

They peered
around closet
doors. They listened
from under curtains and above
the shelves. The friends loved
learning.

THE OUTSIDE

Lunch and recess came quickly. The friends did not go outside. Outside it was cold and snowy.

"If we go out there, we might never get back in," Stella said.

Stella used to live outside. She knew what it was like to be cold, hungry, and lonely. Nico, Delilah, and Bo did not.

Nico used to be a classroom pet. Delilah had hatched in a corner of the teacher's lounge. Bo was from a pet store. He went home with his teacher on weekends.

Now they were together, warm and safe. The school was their home. They were a family. Stella did not want to be cold, hungry, or lonely ever again.

The friends all looked outside.

"The games look fun," said Stella. She had studied how groups work.

"But a storm is coming,"
said Nico. He had studied weather.

"And the clock says they'll come
in soon. Recess is almost over," said
Delilah. She had studied time.

Bo looked at the sky. His wings
twitched. He wanted to fly.

"Maybe I should go outside and
try it," said Bo.

"I don't think that's a good idea," said Stella. "But let's go ask Goldie for some advice."

Whenever the friends didn't know what to do, they went to see Goldie the Goldfish. She lived in the media center. Goldie was very wise.

"Goldie, should Bo go outside?" asked Stella.

Goldie swam in a circle.

"Blub, blub," she said.

One blub meant "yes." Two blubs meant "no." At least, that's what the friends thought she meant.

"She's right," said Stella.
"Outside you would be cold,
hungry, and lonely."

"True," Bo said. "Plus I love to
read. There are no books outside."

THE END

The children ran inside from recess. Their cheeks were red. Their voices were happy. They went back to class.

The animals were ready and waiting. They loved the afternoon at school. There were so many fun subjects.

Stella loved music class because she could sing. She could only run across the piano keys at night.

Nico loved art class. He painted with his toes. Blue was his color of choice in winter.

Delilah loved the computer lab. She was learning to code.

Bo loved the library. He read stories. He read poems. He read the entire dinosaur section TWICE!

Gym class was not safe for small animals. Balls flew and feet pounded.

The friends watched and tried to stay safe. It wasn't easy!

At the end of the day, the children packed their backpacks and left. They stomped out the front doors and climbed up the bus steps.

The kids were always happy to be done with the school day. Stella didn't understand why, since she thought it was so fun.

Stella watched from the window and sniffled a little. The school was so quiet with no children.

"Come on, Stella," said Nico.

"The broom will come soon," said Delilah.

"And after the broom goes," said Bo, "we can go play the piano."

Stella smiled. Even without the children, she wasn't lonely. She had her friends. She had a home.

And besides, tomorrow the children would be back. Tomorrow the school would be bright and loud again.

Brinnnnng! went the final bell.

TALK ABOUT IT

1. Each character has a different personality. Which one of the school sidekicks would you be? Why?

2. This story takes place in winter. What words and illustrations showed that?

3. Talk about your favorite subject in school (besides lunch and recess).

WRITE ABOUT IT

1. Go through the story and write down the schedule the children followed through the day. Compare it to your school schedule.

2. The five animals in this story are best friends. Write a paragraph about your best friends.

3. Pretend you're Goldie, and write a journal entry about your day.

MOLLY BETH GRIFFIN

Molly Beth Griffin is a writing teacher at the Loft Literary Center in Minneapolis, Minnesota. She has written numerous picture books (including *Loon Baby* and *Rhoda's Rock Hunt*) and a YA novel *(Silhouette of a Sparrow)*. Molly loves reading and hiking in all kinds of weather. She lives in South Minneapolis with her partner and two kids.

COLIN JACK

Colin Jack has illustrated several books for children, including *Little Miss Muffet* (Flip-Side Rhymes), *Jack and Jill* (Flip-Side Rhymes), *Dragons from Mars*, *7 Days of Awesome*, and *If You Happen to Have a Dinosaur*. He also works as a story artist and character designer at DreamWorks Studios. Colin splits his time living in California and Canada with his wife and two children.

PLENTY OF SIDEKICK FUN!

Discover more at
www.capstonekids.com

School Sidekicks is published by
Picture Window Books, a Capstone Imprint
1710 Roe Crest Drive, North Mankato, Minnesota 56003
www.mycapstone.com

Library of Congress Cataloging-in-Publication Data
Names: Griffin, Molly Beth, author. | Jack, Colin, illustrator.
Title: Friends all day / by Molly Beth Griffin ; illustrated by Colin Jack.

Description: North Mankato, Minnesota : Picture Window Books, [2019]
| Series: Picture Window Books. School sidekicks |

Summary: Stella the Mouse, Nico the Toad, Delilah the Spider, and Bo
the Parakeet are four animal friends that live in the school; Stella came
in from the outside, Nico was a classroom pet (until he escaped), Delilah
hatched in a corner of the teacher's lounge, and Bo goes home with
his human (a teacher) on weekends—but they all love watching the
students work and play, and at night they have each other.

Identifiers: LCCN 2018037918 | ISBN 9781515838876 (hardcover) |
ISBN 9781515838913 (ebook pdf)

Subjects: LCSH: Animals—Juvenile fiction. | Elementary schools—
Juvenile fiction. | Friendship—Juvenile fiction. | CYAC: Animals—
Fiction. | Schools—Fiction. | Friendship—Fiction

Classification: LCC PZ7.G8813593 Fr 2019 | DDC 813.6 [E]
dc23LC record available at https://lccn.loc.gov/2018037918

Book design by: Ted Williams
Shutterstock: AVA Bitter, design element throughout,
Oleksandr Rybitskiy, design element throughout

Printed and bound in the United States of America.
PA49